Dear Parent:
Your child's love of reading starts here!

Every child learns to read in a different way and at his or her own speed. Some go back and forth between reading levels and read favorite books again and again. Others read through each level in order. You can help your young reader improve and become more confident by encouraging his or her own interests and abilities. From books your child reads with you to the first books he or she reads alone, there are I Can Read Books for every stage of reading:

SHARED READING
Basic language, word repetition, and whimsical illustrations, ideal for sharing with your emergent reader

BEGINNING READING
Short sentences, familiar words, and simple concepts for children eager to read on their own

READING WITH HELP
Engaging stories, longer sentences, and language play for developing readers

READING ALONE
Complex plots, challenging vocabulary, and high-interest topics for the independent reader

ADVANCED READING
Short paragraphs, chapters, and exciting themes for the perfect bridge to chapter books

I Can Read Books have introduced children to the joy of reading since 1957. Featuring award-winning authors and illustrators and a fabulous cast of beloved characters, I Can Read Books set the standard for beginning readers.

A lifetime of discovery begins with the magical words **"I Can Read!"**

Visit www.icanread.com for information
on enriching your child's reading experience.

Pony Crazy

For Tamar Mays, Meg Haston,
and pony lovers everywhere
—C.H.

For Dana and all the ponies
at Wilcox Pony Farm
—A.K.

I Can Read Book® is a trademark of HarperCollins Publishers.

Pony Scouts: Pony Crazy copyright © 2008 by HarperCollins Publishers All rights reserved. Manufactured in China. No part of this book may be used or reproduced in any manner whatsoever without written permission except in the case of brief quotations embodied in critical articles and reviews. For information address HarperCollins Children's Books, a division of HarperCollins Publishers, 10 East 53rd Street, New York, NY 10022. www.icanread.com

Library of Congress catalog card number: 2007942470
ISBN 978-0-06-125533-5 (trade bdg.) — ISBN 978-0-06-125535-9 (pbk.)

❖

10 11 12 13 14   SCP   10 9 8 7 6 5 4 3 2
First Edition

Pony Crazy

story by Catherine Hapka
pictures by Anne Kennedy

HARPER
An Imprint of HarperCollinsPublishers

Meg loved horses.

She thought about horses,

she talked about horses,

and she drew pictures of horses.

Meg lived in the big city.

There were no horses there.

Then something exciting happened.

Meg's family moved to the country!

Meg got to school early
on her first day.
"Welcome to Little Creek School,"
said her teacher.
"I hope you like it here."
She showed Meg to her desk.

It was show-and-tell day

so Meg had brought her best horse.

"Hi," said the girl next to Meg.

"I'm Jill. I like your pony."

Meg smiled. "Her name is Moonbeam.

And my name is Meg."

"Moonbeam is a pretty name,"
said Jill.

"She looks like my mom's pony, Sparkle."

"Your mom has a real pony?" Meg asked.

The teacher started class
before Meg could ask more questions.
"Say hello to Meg!" the teacher said.
"This is her first day.
Meg, please go first
for show-and-tell."

Meg stood in front of the class.

"Moonbeam is my favorite horse,"

she told the class.

"I wish I had a real pony!"

That afternoon,

Jill found her mother in the barn.

She was mucking out a pony's stall.

Jill patted the nose
of her favorite pony, Apples.
"Hey, Mom," she said.
"I made a new friend today.
Can she come over?"

"Guess what!" Jill said

the next day at school.

"My mom says I can invite you over

to meet the ponies!

My friend Annie is coming, too!"

Meg was very excited.

She called to ask her parents

if she could go to Jill's house.

They said yes!

School seemed to last forever.

But soon the bell rang.

"It's pony time!" Meg said.

Jill's mom was waiting in the barn.

"Hello, girls," she said.

"I hear you like ponies."

"Like them?" Meg laughed.

"I love them!"

"This is Apples," Jill said,
patting a cute chestnut pony.
"He's my favorite."
"Oh!" Meg cried.
"His nose is so soft!"

"My sister got to ride a pony
with her scout troop," said Annie.
"They earned a cool badge."
The girls met Inky and Smoky,
two black ponies.

Next the girls met Sparkle,

the pretty gray pony

that looked just like Moonbeam.

They also met Splash,

a brown-and-white pony.

Annie giggled. "Splash is cute!

I like his spots."

"Spotted ponies are called pintos,"
Jill's mom said.

The girls patted the ponies
and fed them apples and mints.
"Who wants hot chocolate?"
Jill's mom asked after a while.

Soon the three girls were sitting

at the table inside Jill's house.

"This was fun," Jill said.

After that,

all three of them spoke at once.

"I wish we could get together again,"
Jill said.

"I wish I could see
the ponies more often," Meg said.

"I wish the three of us
were a scout troop," Annie said.

They all looked at one another.

Jill's mom smiled.

"It sounds like you girls

just had a great idea," she said.

"We did?" Jill said.

"What was it?"

Her mom laughed.

"You three could be

the Pony Scouts!"

"The Pony Scouts!"

the three girls cried.

"We can earn ribbons," Annie said.

"And hang out together," Jill added.

"And play with ponies!" Meg cried.

And that's exactly
what they decided to do.

PONY POINTERS

stall: a place in a barn where ponies live

mucking out a stall: cleaning a stall

chestnut: The color of a horse or pony that is red-brown all over

pinto: a spotted horse or pony